AF266365


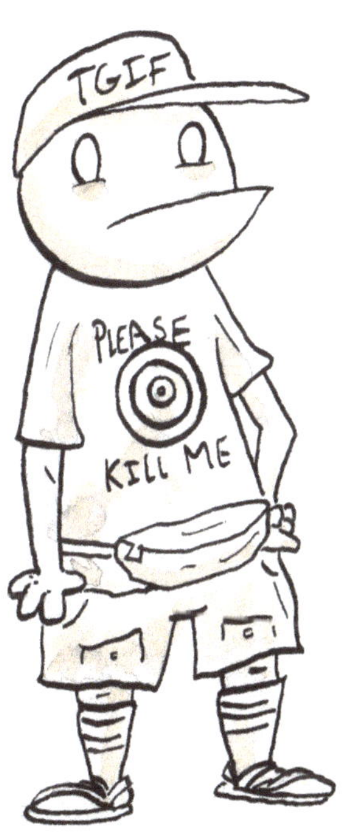

TGIF
PLEASE
KILL ME

# Reason Is Passé

## An Acronyphobic Fluffle

by
Briney Pete

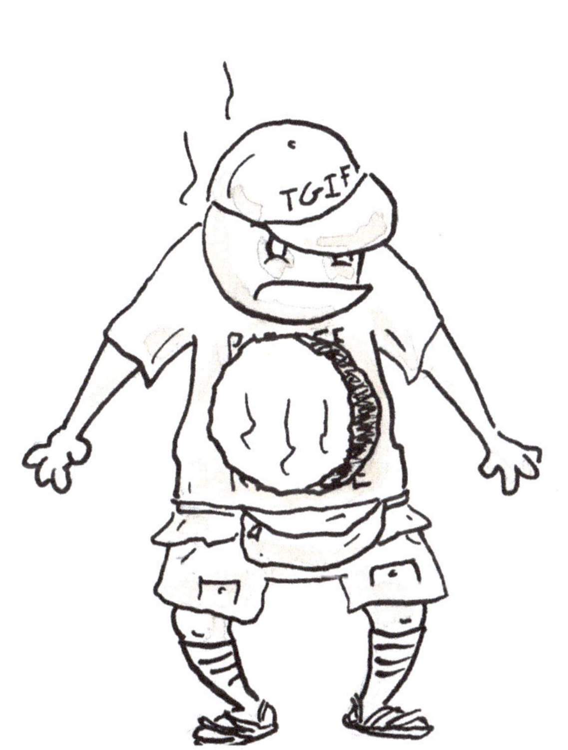
TGIF

# Reason Is Passé
## An Acronyphobic Fluffle
## by Briney Pete



ISBN: 978-1-946296-05-4

I can hear baby birds living in the roof just above my desk, which means this first printing must be late spring 2018.

All acronyms contained in this book were used with the explicit permission of the internet.

Never Knows HMC is a company in Olympia, WA and is definitely not a pyramid scheme even a little.

Calavara.com
NeverKnows.com

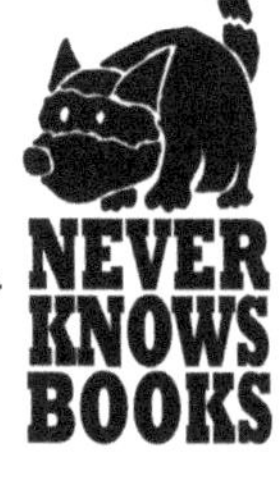

Dedicated to
Stephanie Johnson,
Olympia's Queen of Acronyms

# 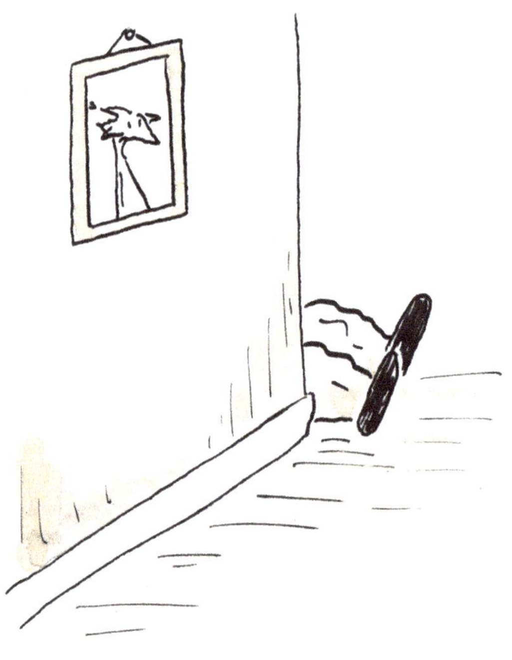

Alison went AWOL, and she's probably now dead.

# $B$en said "BRB" just before going off his meds.

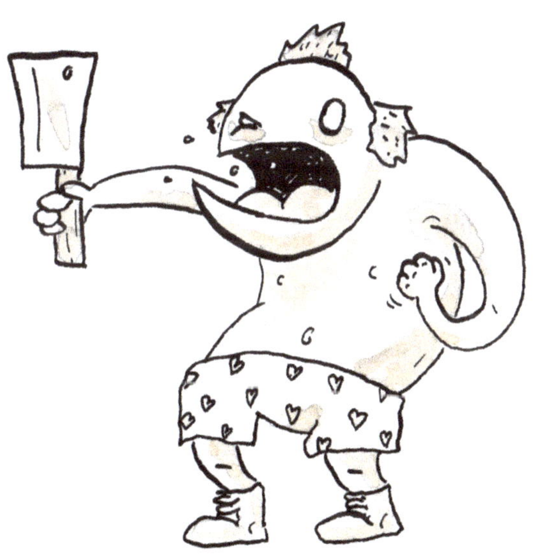

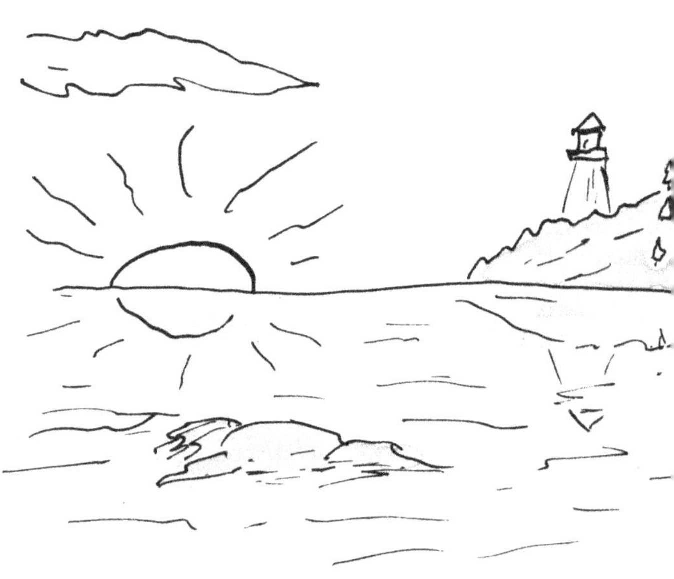

Chad lied to the CIA until he turned up in the bay.

# Donna came to visit but she showed up DOA.

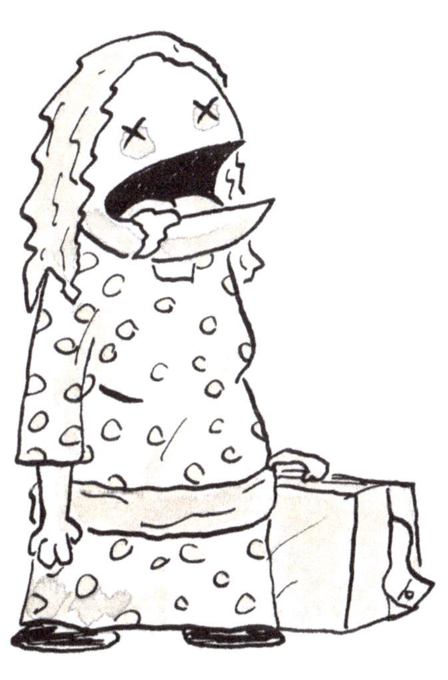

Em was ESL and so she couldn't read the warning.

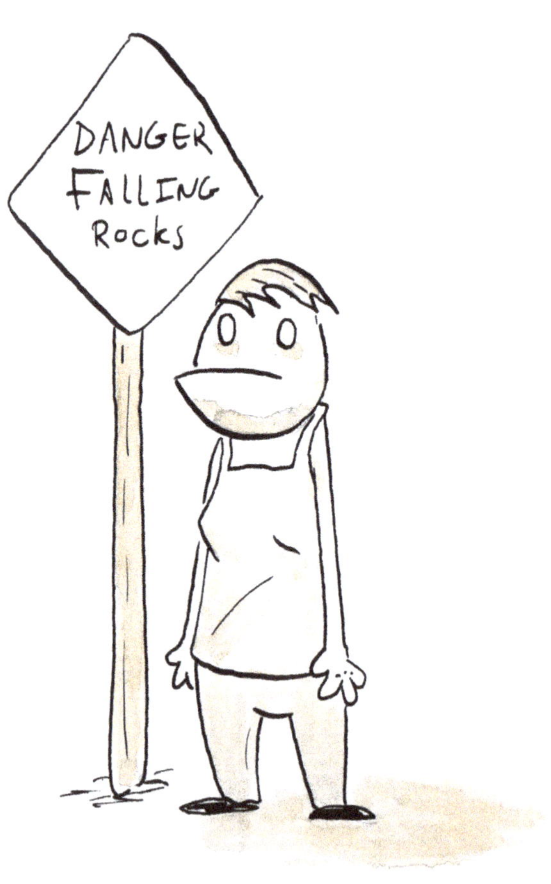

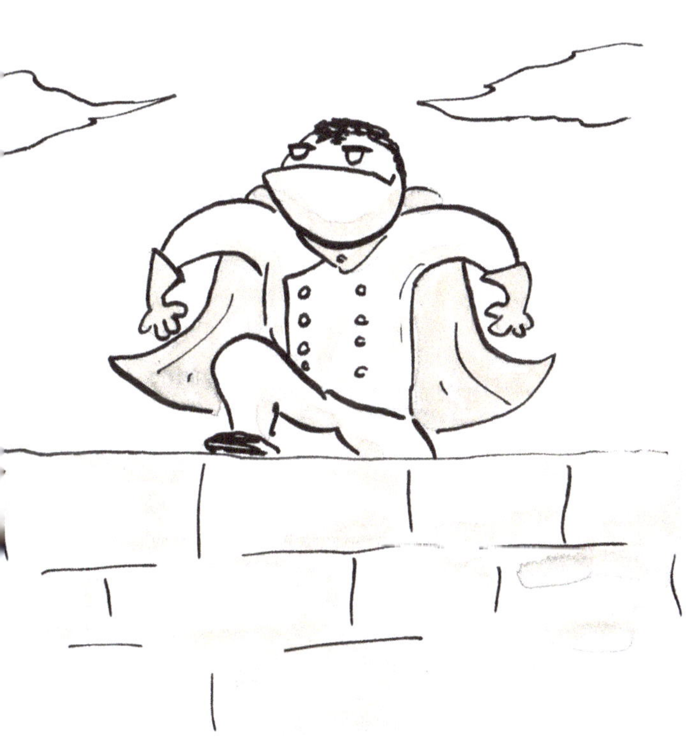


F rank said "FTW!"
and then leapt off the
roof one morning.

Greg's GF loved him
too much and he should
have chose to flee.

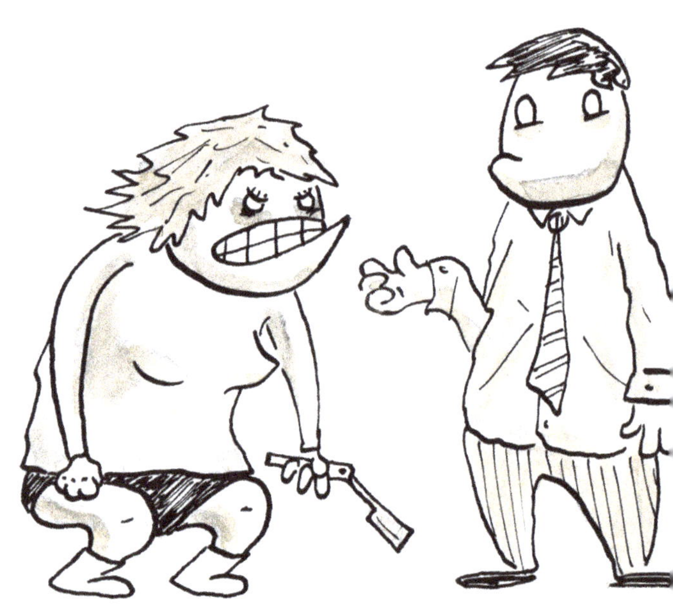

# Henry's death was imminent, his HMO did not agree.

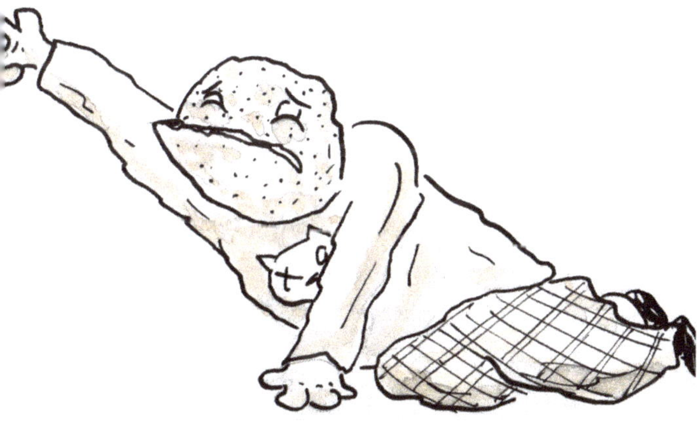

"IDK" declared Imelda when she was asked what made her sick.

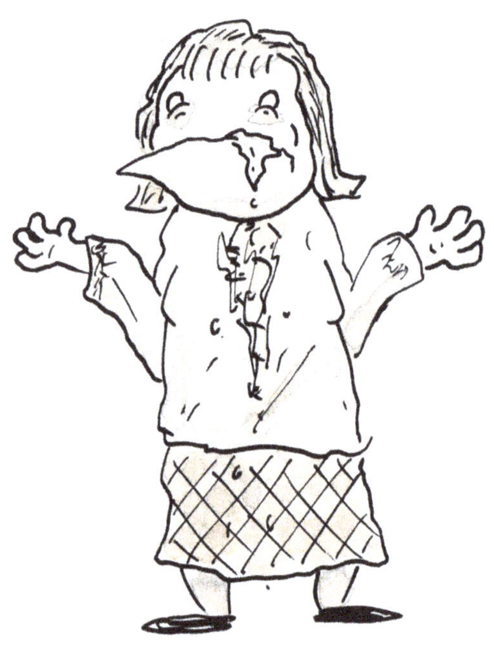

$J$ustin said "JK" and then was crushed under some bricks.

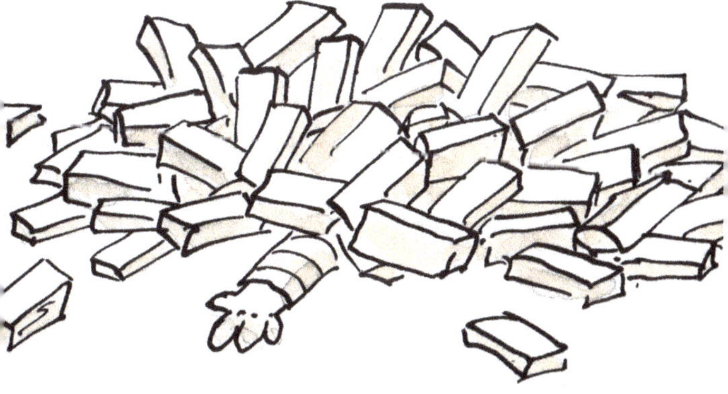

Kay couldn't have known that she would never KIT.

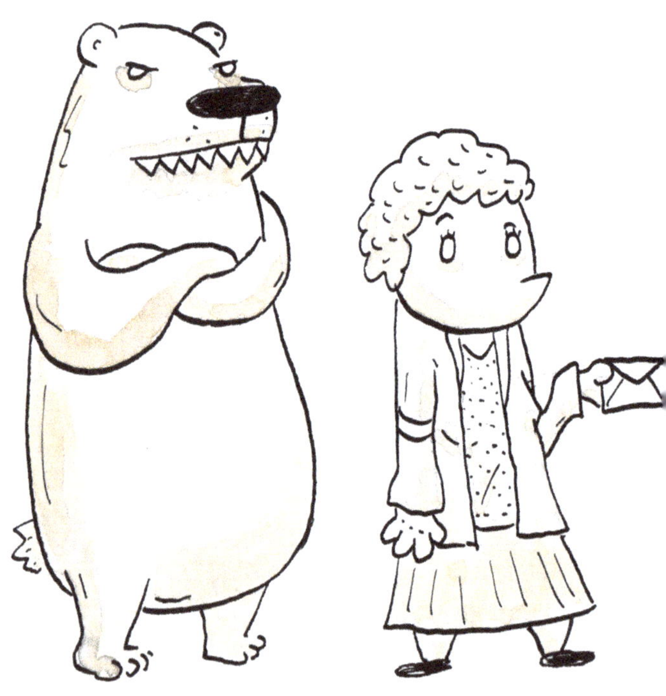

Lou said "LOL" and
then a clown broke
both his knees.

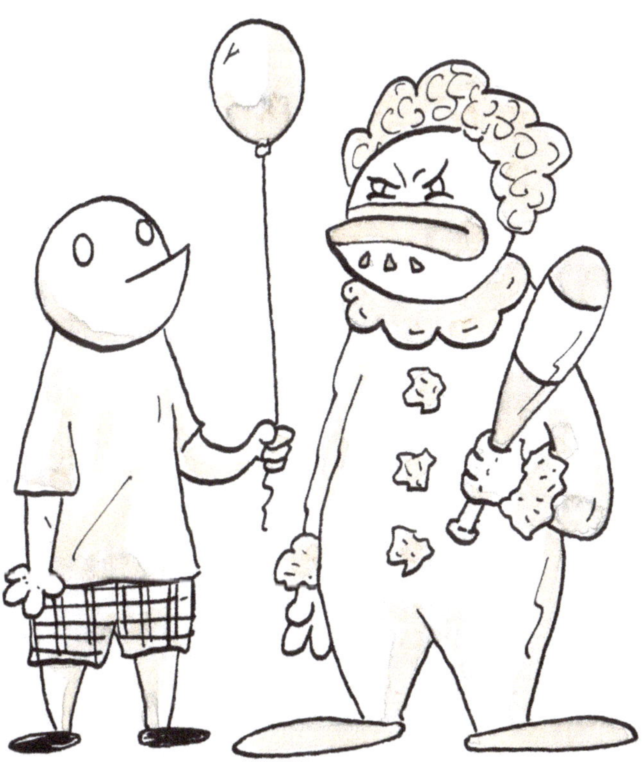

Min was MIA as she had always warned she'd be.

# Ned was NSFW as you can plainly see.

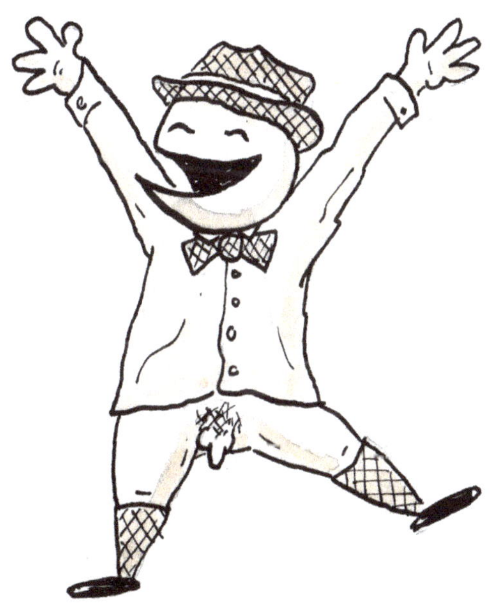

Oscar kept saying OMG until he made the big guy mad.

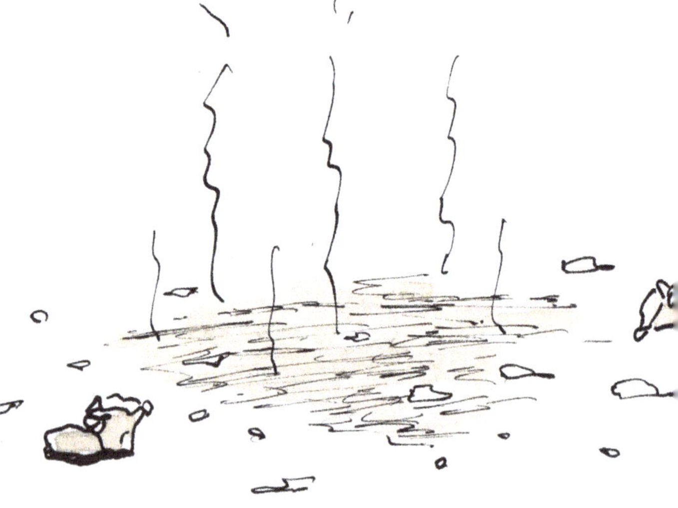

Ping learned that the PTA was run by the triad.

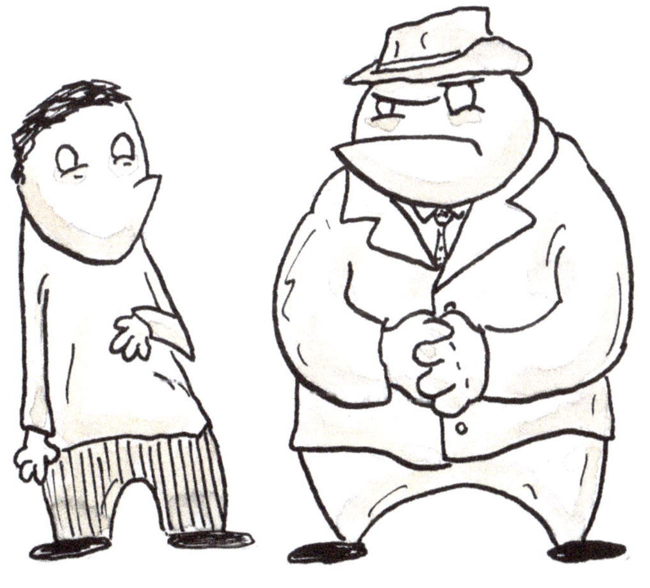

Queenie's every dumb pronouncement was concluded QED.

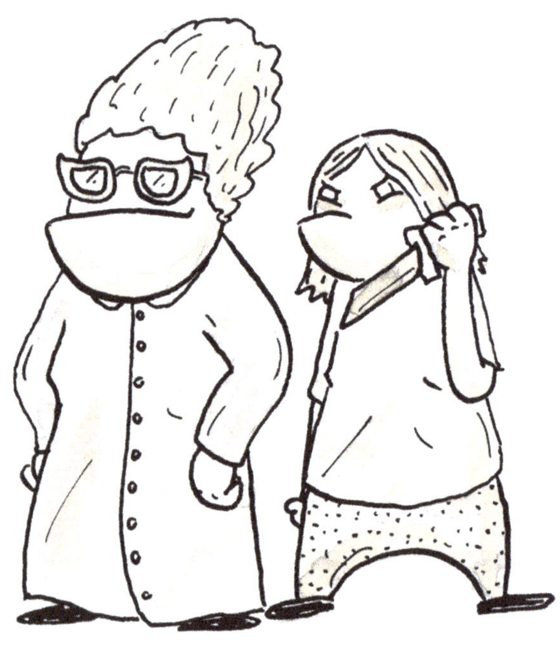

# Ralph ROFL'd until he rolled off a cliff into the sea.

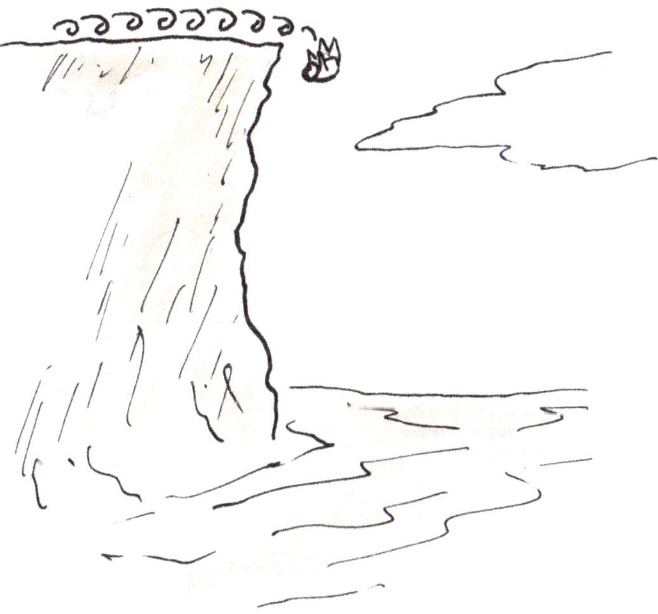

"STFU Sammy"
was written on the
wall in blood.

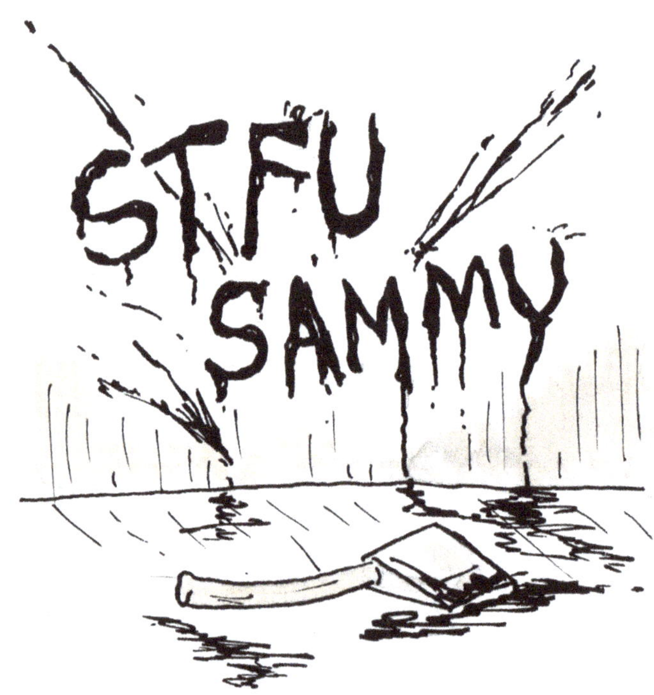

Troy said "TL/DR" and then was washed off by the flood.

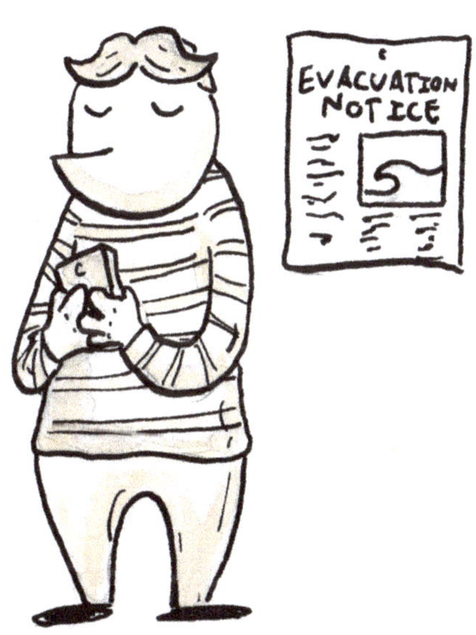

# Uma saw a UFO which made her fall out of a tree.

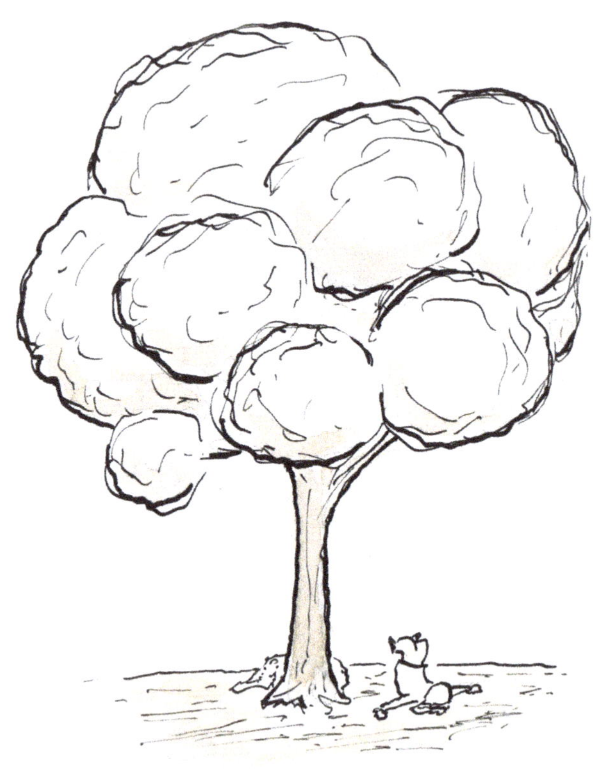

Vicky thought she
was a VIP, the wolves
did not agree.

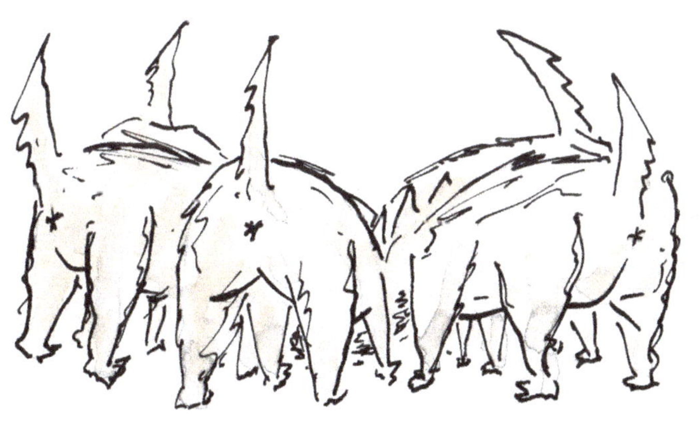

"WWJD" screamed Winn as he was sentenced by the king.

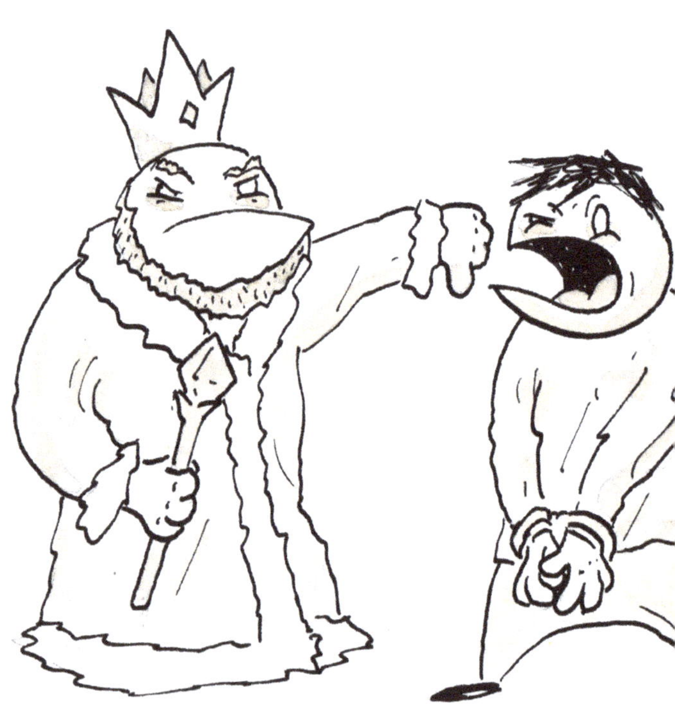

# Ximon needs to XYZ
## because we all see
### *everything.*

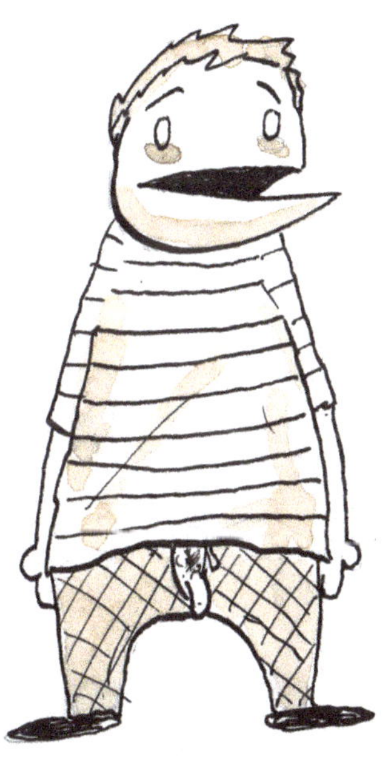

Yolanda shouted "YOLO" and it turns out she was right.

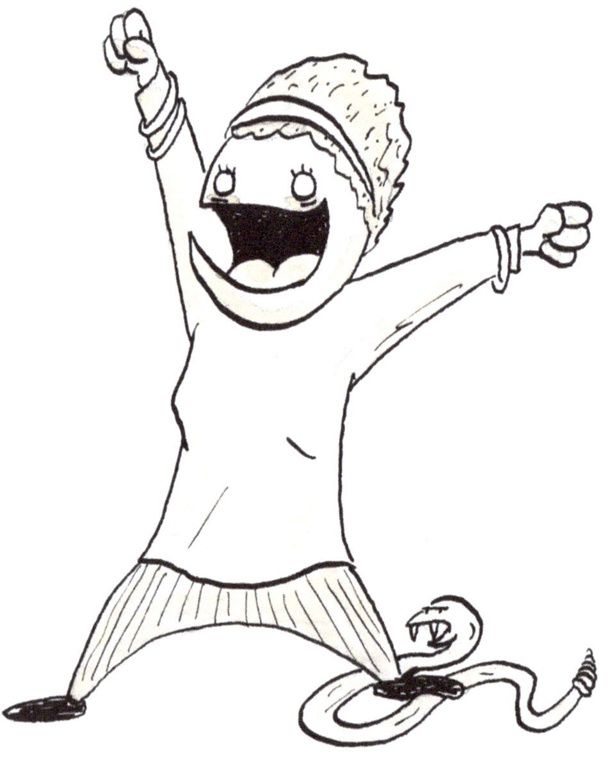

Z oe thought ZZZ was an acronym because she's none too bright.

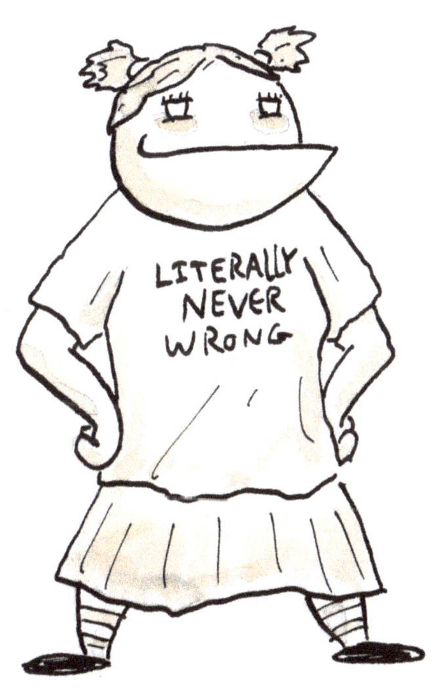

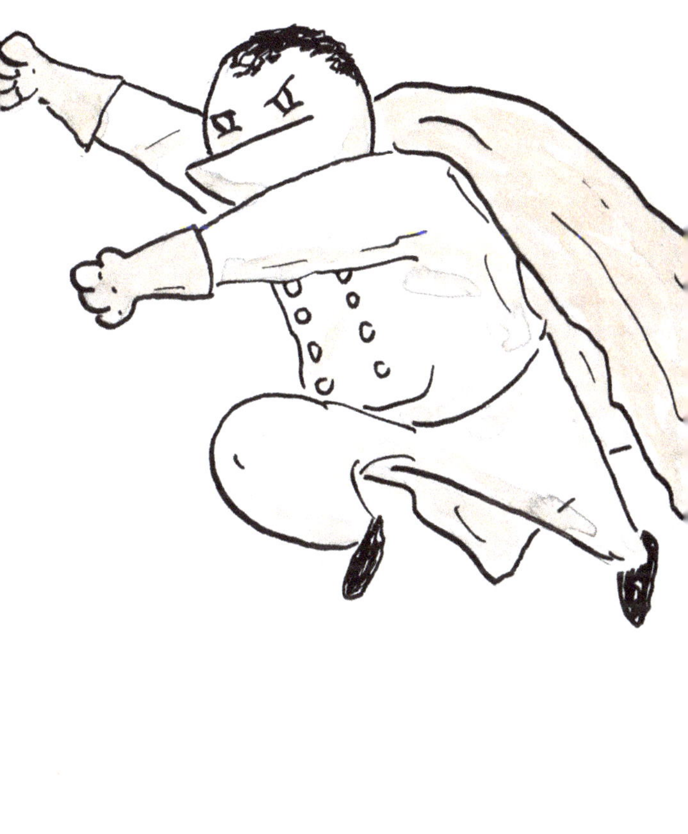

# Glossary For Mom

AWOL - Absent Without Leave

BRB - Be Right Back

CIA - Central Intelligence Agency

DOA - Dead On Arrival

ESL - English as a Second Language

FTW - For The Win, *also* Fuck The World

GF - GirlFriend

HMO - Health Maintenance Organization

IDK - I Don't Know

JK - Just Kidding

KIT - Keep In Touch

LOL - Laugh Out Loud

MIA - Missing In Action

NSFW - Not Safe For Work

OMG - Oh My God

PTA - Parent Teacher Association

QED - Quod Erat Demonstrandum (Latin)
        basically means "as demonstrated"

ROFL - Rolling On the Floor Laughing

STFU - Shut The Fuck Up

TL/DR - Too Long / Didn't Read

UFO - Unidentified Flying Object

VIP - Very Important Person

WWJD - What Would Jesus Do

XYZ - (Check) Your Zipper

YOLO - You Only Live Once

ZZZ - *Not an acronym*

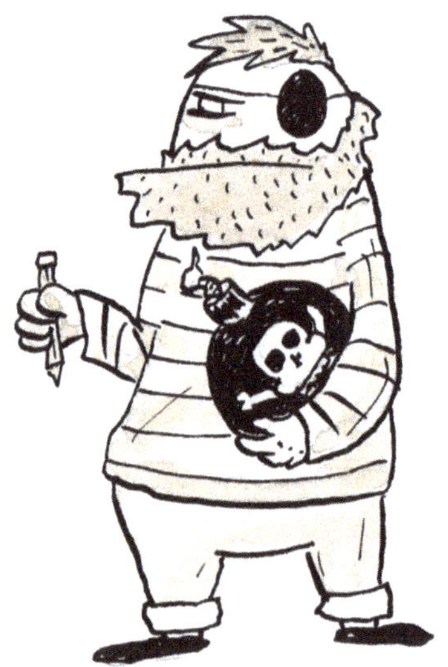

Briney "Pete" Calavara lives in Olympia, WA, when he isn't sailing the high seas, pillaging, and burying shiny things in secret locations that you'll never ever find, nyah nyah nyah nyah. Available for parties and marauding at what I assume are very reasonable rates.